W9-ADO-293

STICKLEY MAKES a MisTake!

A Frog's Guide to Trying Again

by Brenda S. Miles, PhD
illustrated by Steve Mack

Magination Press • Washington, DC
American Psychological Association

for Martha—an extraordinary teacher who transforms ordinary mistakes—BSM

for Erin. Together we've raised some great little tadpoles!—SM

Published by
MAGINATION PRESS ®
An Educational Publishing Foundation Book
American Psychological Association
750 First Street NE
Washington, DC 20002

Magination Press is a registered trademark of the American Psychological Association.

For more information about our books, including a complete catalog,
please write to us, call 1-800-374-2721, or visit our website at www.apa.org/pubs/magination.

Book design by Sandra Kimbell
Printed by Lake Book Manufacturing, Melrose Park, IL

Library of Congress Cataloging-in-Publication Data
Names: Miles, Brenda. | Mack, Steve (Steve Page), illustrator.
Title: Stickley makes a mistake! : a frog's guide to trying again /
by Brenda S. Miles, PhD; illustrated by Steve Mack.
Description: Washington, DC : Magination Press, 2016. | "American
Psychological Association." | Summary: With help from his grandpa,
Stickley the frog, who hates making mistakes, learns to say "oh well,"
hop up, and try again when mistakes happen.
Identifiers: LCCN 2016005289| ISBN 9781433822643 (hardcover) |
ISBN 1433822644 (hardcover)
Subjects: | CYAC: Perseverance (Ethics)—Fiction. | Errors—Fiction. |
Frogs—Fiction. | Animals—Fiction.
Classification: LCC PZ7.M5942 Sr 2016 | DDC [E]—dc23
LC record available at http://lccn.loc.gov/2016005289

Manufactured in the United States of America
10 9 8 7 6 5 4 3 2 1

When Stickley was young, he didn't like making mistakes.
"Oh no!" he'd say, and he wouldn't try again.
He wanted to be perfect.

"But Stickley," said Grandpa. "We're frogs.
We stick to things—even when we make mistakes.
So instead of 'oh no,' say, 'oh well.'"

"And then what?" asked Stickley.

"Look at your mistake—you'll learn something new!
Take a new look at the problem, too!

No one is perfect,
so practice your best!

If you're stuck on a problem,
ask for help with the rest!

Feel proud for trying—that's what to do!
Hop up! Try again! Say 'oh well' to get through!"

When Stickley spelled cat K-A-T, **OOPS!**

"Oh no!" said Stickley.

"Oh well," said Grandpa.
"Look closely and learn something new!"

"Aha!" said Stickley. "There is a K-A-T!
What I want is a C-A-T."

When Stickley was painting,

SPILL! SPLAT!

"Oh no!" he said, but
then he remembered.
"Oh well."

"I'll take a new look!"

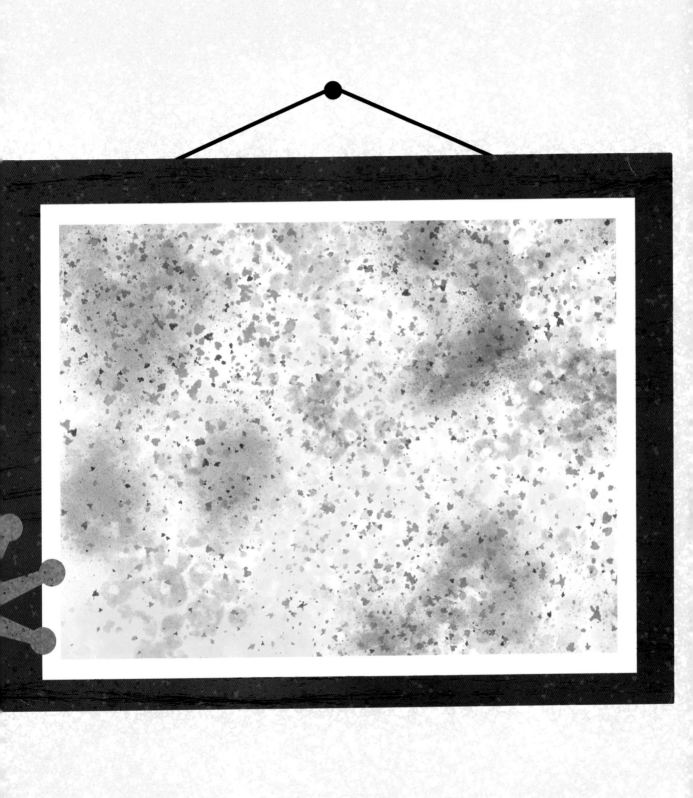

When Stickley played his trumpet,

SCREECH!

"Oh well," said Stickley.

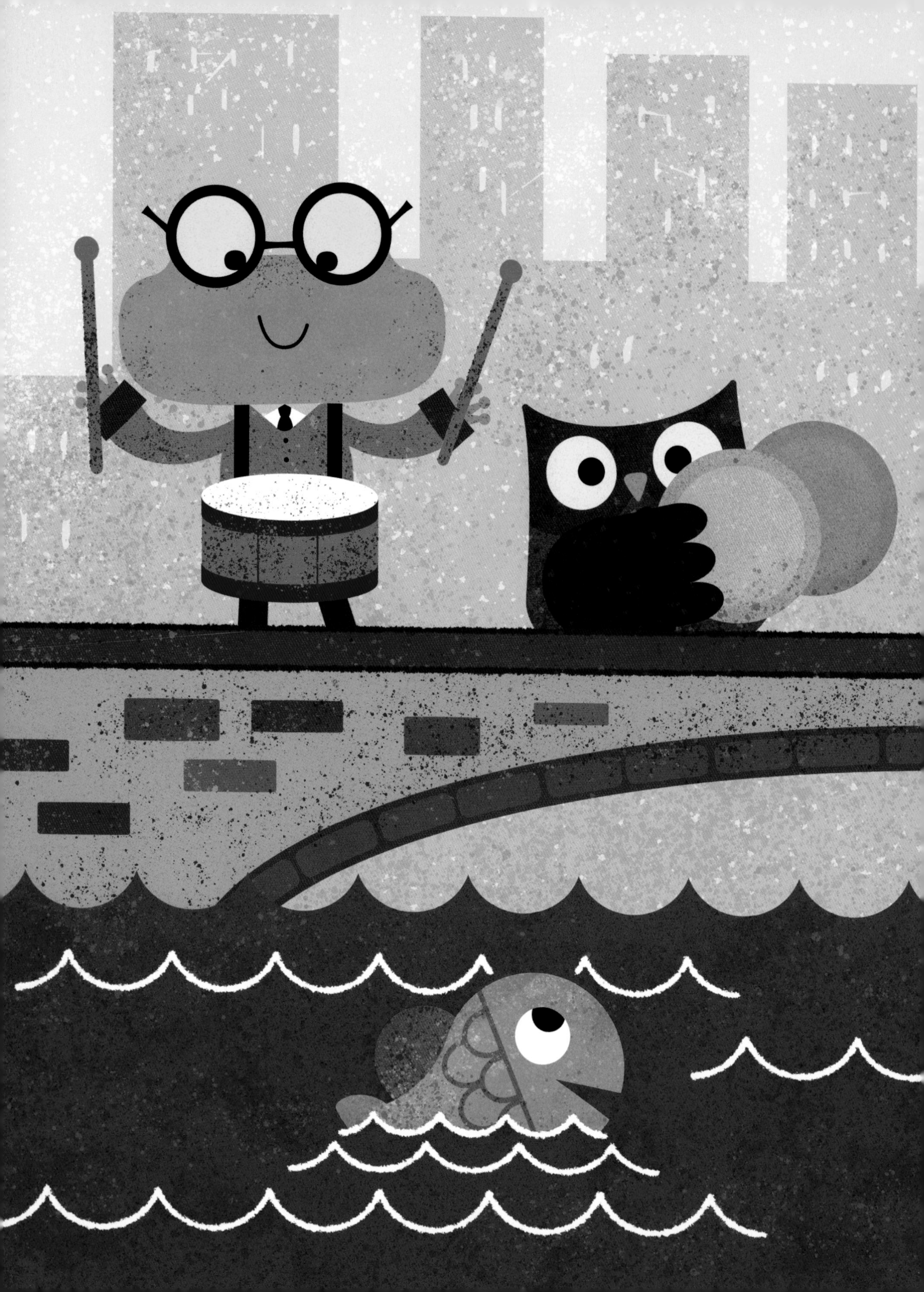

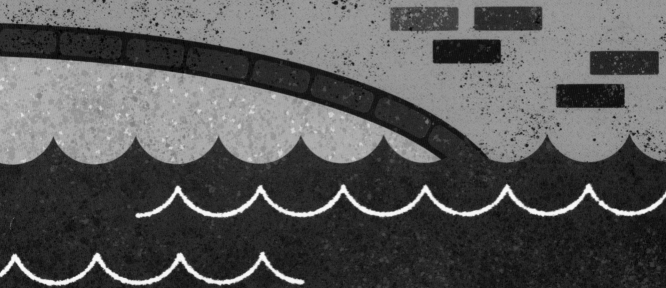

"I'll practice to get better!"

When Stickley wrote 1 + 1 = 3,

aaRGH!

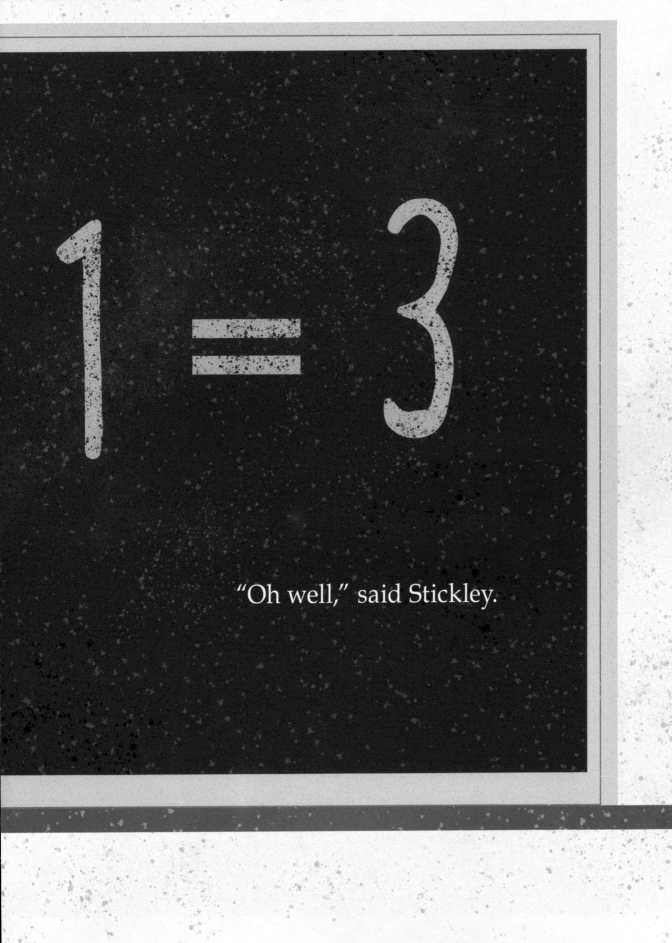

1 = 3

"Oh well," said Stickley.

"It's time to ask for help."

"1 + 1 is 2," said
a polar bear.
"And two scoops of
help is always sweet!"

Stickley tried his best, but mistakes *still* happened.
When he cooked his famous pancakes—another mistake!

PLINK! PLIP!

He used blueberries instead of chocolate chips!

"Oh well," said Stickley. "I'll feel proud for trying."

"YUM!" said Octavia. "This mistake tastes great! Let's celebrate!"

HOORAY!

Nobody's perfect and good things can happen—even when you make mistakes!

Many adults don't like making mistakes—and children are no different. But mistakes happen, and they are a natural and necessary part of growing up. Mistakes help the brain grow when challenges arise. Without mistakes there would be no problem solving. And without problem solving there would be no learning. And without learning there would be no growing up—for adults and children!

Dr. Carol Dweck, a psychologist who studies mistakes, makes an interesting observation. When a toddler first learns to walk, we expect stumbles and falls. Are those falls mistakes or just a normal part of development? Most people would say the toddler is learning rather than making mistakes. From a developmental perspective, that viewpoint makes the most sense. But a curious thing happens as children grow older and become more aware of others around them. Now they see missteps as *mistakes*—potentially catastrophic events causing shame and doubt. This shift in perspective is unfortunate because new learning is tough, if not impossible, when challenges are avoided for the sake of achieving success on easier tasks.

Dr. Dweck argues that adults differ in how they view mistakes—and so do children! Not all people see mistakes as unfortunate events. For some, mistakes are necessary for learning and improving. How we view mistakes determines whether we embrace challenges or avoid them altogether. Children who are willing to learn from mistakes take more risks in their learning, and are more likely to keep trying when challenged, than children who are hesitant to do anything wrong. To learn more about Dr. Dweck's ideas, visit http://mindsetonline.com.

So how do you teach your child that mistakes are great? Here are some strategies to help get you started.

Provide a loving relationship no matter what. Raising a child who is willing to learn from mistakes starts early. By letting your children know that you love them unconditionally—which means *no matter what*—you are teaching them that they can take healthy risks and won't be judged harshly if things don't go as planned. Explain that making mistakes is part of growing up; it's learning from your mistakes that matters. Let your children know you'll be there for them with love and encouragement as they try to figure things out.

Praise effort, not smarts. According to Dr. Dweck's research, it doesn't take much to convince children to steer clear of mistakes. When children solved a problem and were told they were "smart," they chose an easy task the next time instead of a challenging one they might not solve. Why? Because they needed to prove they were smart again by solving the next problem correctly. After all, if they tried a tough task and failed, what would that mean? That they weren't smart anymore? On the other hand, children who were told they had "worked very hard" the first time were more likely to attempt a tougher task the next time. As long as they were still trying, it didn't matter if they got the second problem right. Lesson learned? Praise your children for trying hard, and avoid labels like *smart, brilliant,* or *talented.*

Discuss how the brain learns. Give your child a mini-lesson in brain science. Explain that the brain is made of billions of cells called neurons. As the brain develops, more and more cells "talk to each other" by growing connections. When anyone makes mistakes, or doesn't know how to do something yet, like skate or multiply in math, the brain needs to build new connections, so that neurons can talk to each other. One way to build these connections is to try and solve a problem over and over and over again until the brain finds a solution. After lots of hard work, solving a problem means new connections have formed, telling brain cells what to do. So encourage your child to make mistakes, try again and again, and build brain highways so that finding solutions is easier the next time. Bottom line: brains need mistakes to grow.

Explain that practice makes better, not perfect. For all of us, it's helpful to understand that skills can improve, even when games are lost and mistakes are made. Explain to your child that athletes weren't born shooting hoops, and doctors weren't born knowing how to take care of people. Being an expert in any field—whether in the lab or on the court—isn't about natural talent; it's about hard work. If your child wants to become more skilled at anything, explain that consistent practice is key. Avoid the popular saying, "practice makes perfect," however. Remember, there is no perfect. What's important is effort, not outcome. Reinforce that practice makes better, but not perfect, because new gains bring new challenges. What really counts is consistent effort, a willingness to be less than the best, and the confidence to keep improving.

Explore practice further. Your child might believe that practice is crucial for sports but have a different viewpoint altogether when it comes to learning in school. If your child is hesitant to make mistakes in some areas but not others, explain that practice and effort are important for all tasks. For example, you might say, "practice helped you become a better soccer player—and practice can help you become better at math, too!"

Encourage requests for help. Stickley learns that good things happen when he makes mistakes and chooses to be persistent. One of those good things is getting help when he really needs it. Teach your child that asking for help isn't a bad thing; instead, it's a good thing that helps the brain learn. For tasks that might seem big from the start, don't wait for your child to request help if you know huge frustration is inevitable. Instead, break the task down into manageable chunks and provide a few suggestions for working through the problem at the beginning. Some children may be hesitant to start a task, not because they are afraid of making mistakes, but because they don't know where to begin! So help your child get started on big tasks but don't rush in to solve every problem. Let mistakes happen, and encourage requests for help when your child is truly stuck and feeling frustrated.

Encourage ownership. Mistakes happen to all of us—sometimes on the job, sometimes on the sports field, and sometimes in our friendships. Teach your child to take ownership and not blame others when mistakes occur. That means admitting that *you* made the mistake, and that no one else is to blame. Then problem solve how to make things right. Maybe it's studying harder for a test the next time, practicing more before the next tournament, or saying "sorry" to a friend for hurting his or her feelings. In the case of moral mistakes, like cheating or being unkind, explain that you love your child but that these kinds of mistakes—ones that are dishonest or hurtful—are unacceptable and must be addressed with a positive action, like an apology, to help correct the wrong-doing. Explain that mistakes happen, but what you learn from those mistakes, and how you respond to them, are most important.

Help change the tone. Help change the tone from shame to pride, at least for mistakes in learning, sports, or other ventures that involve taking healthy risks. Explain that nobody's perfect and it takes courage to try new things, especially when you're not sure how those things will turn out. Let your child know that he or she should feel proud for taking chances, learning from mistakes, and trying again.

Teach Grandpa's "oh well" strategy. Stickley's Grandpa says, "Don't say, 'Oh no!' Say, 'Oh well,'" and then leap into a new plan for persistence! Practice this strategy with your child. When your child makes a mistake, change "oh no" to "oh well," and brainstorm what comes next to help move forward. Maybe it's trying again, or asking for help, or looking at the problem in a new way.

Seek support. If your child is experiencing distress over mistakes that seems bigger than expected for your child's age and developmental stage, seek the support of a licensed professional, such as your family doctor or a psychologist or psychiatrist, for further suggestions.

About the Author

Brenda S. Miles, PhD, is a pediatric neuropsychologist who has worked in hospital, rehabilitation, and school settings. She is an author and coauthor of several books for children, including *Princess Penelopea Hates Peas: A Tale of Picky Eating and Avoiding Catastropeas, Move Your Mood!,* and the first Stickley story, *Stickley Sticks to It!: A Frog's Guide to Getting Things Done.* Fun fact: Stickley was inspired by a tiny tree frog Brenda met in her favorite writing spot, St. Simons Island, Georgia.

About the Illustrator

Steve Mack grew up a prairie boy on Canada's Great Plains and has drawn for as long as he can remember. His first lessons in art were taught to him by watching his grandfather do paint-by-numbers at the summer cottage. He has worked for greeting card companies and has illustrated several books. Steve lives in a beautiful valley in a turn-of-the-century farmhouse with his wife and two children. Steve and his children love catching frogs by the river close to their house. They haven't found any frogs with Bermuda shorts on yet…

About Magination Press

Magination Press is an imprint of the American Psychological Association, the largest scientific and professional organization representing psychologists in the United States and the largest association of psychologists worldwide.